Martin Waddell

Napper Goes For Goal

Illustrated by Barrie Mitchell

Puffin Books

PUFFIN BOOKS

Published by the Penguin Group
Penguin Books Ltd, 27 Wrights Lane, London W8 5TZ, England
Penguin Books USA Inc., 375 Hudson Street, New York, New York 10014, USA
Penguin Books Australia Ltd, Ringwood, Victoria, Australia
Penguin Books Canada Ltd, 10 Alcorn Avenue, Toronto, Ontario, Canada M4V 3B2
Penguin Books (NZ) Ltd, 182–190 Wairau Road, Auckland 10, New Zealand

Penguin Books Ltd, Registered Offices: Harmondsworth, Middlesex, England

Published in Puffin Books 1981
20 19 18 17 16 15 14 13 12

Printed in England by Clays Ltd, St Ives plc
Set in Monotype Imprint

A book inspired by

Luke
Nicky
Paul
Paul
Terence
Mark
Stephen
Tony
Colin
Joseph
Conor
Freddie
Robert
Peter and Sister Francis
And everyone connected with St Anne's Primary
School football team.

Contents

Contents

1. The Cubs Against the Stringy Pants

This is our team, Red Row Stars:

Top row (L. to R.): J. Small   P. Scott   S. Rodgers   T. Prince
D. Wilson   A. Watts   H. Haxwell
Bottom row: M. Bellow   H. Brown   N. McCann
C. Small   D. Forbes

I am the one in the middle with the ball and the goofy one next to me is Cyril Small. The goalie is Terence Prince and the one with the hair is Harpur Brown, our schemer. We are the Super Stars of Red Row team. I am Napper McCann and I usually get most of the goals because I have a terrific hard bullet shot WHAM! that beats goalies.

Red Row Stars is what we call our team now, but a year ago we hadn't got a team. We only got one because the Stringy Pants started calling us names and saying we were soft as toffee, because we come from a small school. Then we got our team and they challenged us and they weren't so sure we were soft when we had finished with them!

It started one Saturday morning when we had gone up to the Rec. field where the Stringy Pants were thumping Maypoleleaf Cubs in the Junior Cup. The Stringy Pants are really St Gabriel's Primary from Canal Street, but we call them the Stringy Pants because they used to have special pants and the string broke and the pants fell off. Here is a picture of a Stringy Pants with his pants falling off:

The game between the Stringy Pants and the Maypoleleaf Cubs wasn't much of a game. Most of the Stringy Pants were bigger than the Cubs and they kept hitting the ball up in the air where the poor little Cubs could only watch it floating over their heads. They kept shooting for the top of the goal where the Cub goalie couldn't reach the ball.

'The referee ought to lower the crossbar!' said Terence, who always keeps a special eye on goal-keepers through being a bit of a shot stopper himself.

'It isn't fair,' I said. 'It isn't the Cubs' fault that their goalie is too small to reach high shots. It means the Cubs have no chance at all.'

'It *is* the Cubs' fault,' said Cyril. 'They shouldn't have put one of their small players in goal. You can't expect the Stringy Pants to keep the ball on the ground and give the goalie a chance to reach it, can you?'

'It's still not fair,' I said. 'Some of the Cubs are good players. It's the same old thing. The Stringy Pants win their games because they are bigger than anybody else around here. And they only manage to have bigger players because they have so many more boys to choose from at their school.'

'It isn't their fault that they have a bigger team than anybody else,' Terence said. 'You can't expect them *not* to try to win, can you? If it was windy, you would use the wind, wouldn't you? And if the sun was in the goalie's eyes, you'd lob him. So if the Cub goalie is too small to reach high shots, it's good tactics to hit the ball over his head.'

The ball came down the right wing. The Cub left-back made a lunge for it and missed. That left Gerry Cleland, the St Gabriel's centre-forward, with a clear run at goal. The Cub goalie came out very quickly, narrowing the angle, and forcing Gerry to shoot before he was ready to. Here is the Cub goalie rushing out to narrow the angle:

Gerry shot hurriedly, but it was a good shot. It was hard and low and heading for the far post, but the Cub goalie anticipated where it was going and got down to it. He hung on, and brought the ball down cleanly against his chest. It was a Super Save, and everybody clapped him, including the St Gabriel's referee, Mr Thompson, who wasn't supposed to take sides. But almost the best thing about it was what the goalie did next.

This was the position when the Cub goalie got the ball:

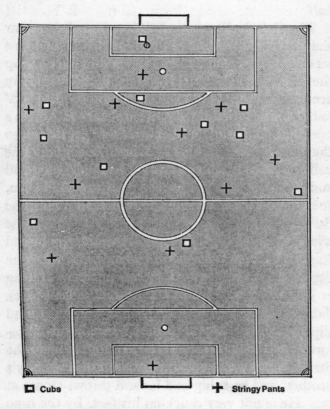

◻ Cubs   **✚ Stringy Pants**

The whole Stringy Pants team had come forward fast, thinking that they were going to score a goal. The right-back had come further than most of them, principally because he is Knocker Lewis, and

Knocker likes scoring goals, and doesn't like being a defender. He had come so far that he left the Cub left-winger unmarked, just inside his own half.

The Cub goalie got up holding the ball, and saw that Knocker was out of position. He didn't need a second look. He cleared the ball, very quickly, up the left wing. It was a neat drop-kick clearance, very accurate, and it fell just inside the Stringy Pants' half of the field, going well over Knocker Lewis's head. It landed in front of the winger and close to the touchline. The Cub winger streaked on to the ball while Knocker Lewis was still turning round and wondering what was happening behind him. Joe Fish, who was playing centre-half for the Stringy Pants, came running across to cut the winger off. Joe is a sensible player, and he had stayed back, in case there was a break-away. But the Stringy Pants' left-back wasn't as quick-thinking as Joe Fish. When Joe moved across, the left-back didn't cover him. The Cub winger saw the gap and slipped the ball inside to his unmarked centre-forward, who was left with only Hugh Cleland, the Stringy Pants' goalkeeper, to beat. Hugh is Gerry's brother, and he is big and fat and throws stones at cats. He is not very quick on his feet. By the time Hugh had made up his mind to come out of goal the Cub centre-forward had reached the ball. He hit it hard and low and it smacked against the upright and zonked into the net.

GOAL!

This is what the Cubs did, from the time the goalkeeper cleared the ball:

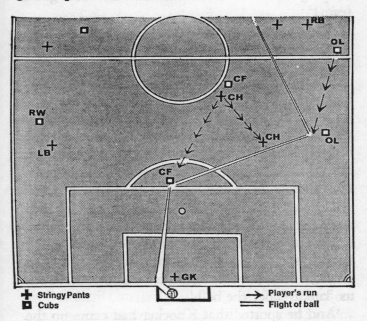

The little arrows mark where the players ran and the lines show the flight of the ball.

'Yah! Cubs forever! Stringy Pants are no good!' we all shouted, but then the final whistle went and it was 4–1 to the Stringy Pants.

'Offside, that was,' Knocker Lewis grumbled, as we walked past him.

'You're wrong, Knocker,' Cyril said. 'The centre-forward was behind the ball when it was played. He ran on to it afterwards!'

'What do you know about it?' Knocker said, whirling round. 'Red Row Kids. You know nothing about football. You haven't even got a team!'

And off he went, looking very cross.

Nobody said anything about it. The thing was, Knocker was right. We had no team.

'The Cub goalie was too small.' I said. 'I would have smashed trillions past him if I'd been playing.'

'He's a decent goalie, though,' said Terence, who always likes talking about goalies, because he is one himself. He has to be a goalie because of his asthma, but I think he might have been one anyway because he is india-rubber and makes Super Saves. 'Look at the way he forced Gerry Cleland to miss. He came out and really put pressure on him. When the ball went down to the other end dozy old Hugh Cleland stayed on his line picking daisies, and when he did realize that he should have come out, it was too late to block the ball.'

'And he spotted that Knocker had come up the field goal-hunting,' Cyril said, talking about the Cubs' goalie again. 'He was clever to see that the left-winger was free to start an attack.'

'He'll be quite a good keeper when he gets taller,' Terence said.

'They only have two tall players in the Cubs,' said Cyril. 'One of them was sick, and the other is the big red-haired one from Mill Street, and you couldn't put him in goal. He keeps falling over and getting his legs wound round lamp-posts that aren't there!'

'Yes,' said Terence.

'You need lots of big players if you're going to have a good team,' said Cyril, and from the way he said it you could tell that he hadn't forgotten what Knocker Lewis had said. We might say the Stringy Pants were no good, but at least they had a team!

'The Stringy Pants may be big,' I said. 'But they can't play football for squashy old black bananas!'

'I wish I went to St Gabriel's,' said Cyril, suddenly. 'I'm fed up with them calling us names!'

'You don't wish you went to St Gabriel's,' said Terence. 'Nobody could wish that. Red Row is Top School, and you know it.'

'We can't even raise a football team,' said Cyril. 'I don't call that being Top School, when we can't even raise a football team.'

It was then that I had my great stupendous exciting idea. I took a deep breath and said:

'WHY NOT?'

'Because we haven't got enough players, that's why not,' said Cyril.

'We've got more than eleven,' I said. 'That's all we need.'

'Not big players,' said Cyril.

'That goalie wasn't big,' said Terence thoughtfully.

'And he lost them the game, because all the goals went in over his head!' said Cyril, triumphantly.

'Terence wouldn't let in goals like that,' I said. 'Being small doesn't matter so much if you are not a goalie.'

'It does matter, though,' said Cyril.

'A lot of the Cubs were smaller than the fifth years. I don't see why we shouldn't have a football team if the Cubs can!' Terence said.

It was at that moment that we really began to believe that we could have a team at Red Row Primary, our first team ever!

'It would be no use having a team full of fourth and fifth years,' Cyril said.

'Better than no team at all!' I said. 'I'm tired of the Clelands and Knocker Lewis going on about their great team, just because they go to a bigger school than we do!'

'We couldn't play little titchy kids against the Stringy Pants,' said Cyril. 'They would make us look silly and get bags of goals and they would be blowing about it forever and calling us names.'

'They do that anyway,' Terence said. 'And some of the little kids aren't so bad. Have you seen Dribbler Wilson in the yard? He could dribble round anyone!'

'I'm not going to play in a silly team with little kids like Wilson,' said Cyril.

There was a silence.

'OK, Cyril. We'll count you out then,' said Terence.

Terence said it very calmly, but really he was taking a big gamble with the whole future of our football team. If Cyril refused to play we couldn't have a team, because Cyril is one of our best players.

'We'll just have to make do without you, Cyril,' Terence said.

Cyril gaped at him. I knew what he was thinking. If there was a team, and C. Small wasn't on it, he was going to look very silly. Cyril is big, despite his name, and very strong, and he is always boasting about playing for Man. United when he grows up.

'I *might* play, I suppose,' he said.

LOST
SCHOOL SCARF
IF FOUND
PLEASE TAKE
TO MISS FOWLER.

RED ROW STARS
EMERGENCY
MEETING
TO FORM A
FOOTBALL
TEAM
BICYCLE SHED
3PM TODAY

Terence winked at me. We had won!

'That's not good enough, Cyril,' I said. 'Make up your mind. Do you want to play on our team, or don't you?'

He finally muttered 'Yes' so off we went to call an emergency meeting and plan the first ever team to represent Red Row Primary School!

'You're bonkers!' my sister Avril said, when she saw our notice on the board. 'You can't go having a football team! You haven't enough players.'

'They'll have to put babies from the fourth year in,' said Ugly Irma Bankworth, who is my sister's rotten friend.

'Will there be girls in it?' asked Helena Bellow.

'You needn't think we're going to play in your stupid team!' said Ugly Irma, quickly.

'We're not,' said Avril. 'We are ladies.'

'We're not going to ask you,' I said.

'Good,' said Irma.

'Good,' said Avril.

Helena didn't say anything, but later she came up to me in the P6 and P7 room and said: 'I'm a better footballer than my brother Marky.'

'Marky is a puddin',' Cyril Small said.

But we decided we couldn't have Helena in our team, because the Stringy Pants would make jokes about us. It was a pity because Helena was a better player than Marky, and we could have used her as substitute.

'They'd call us Knickers United,' Cyril said.

So we decided ours had to be a No-Girls team, even if we had more girls than boys in P6 and P7.

'I didn't want to play anyway,' Helena said, but she did really.

2. The Form-a-football-team Meeting

'I call the meeting to order,' said Terence Prince.

'What does that mean?' asked Harpur Brown.

'Shut up, Harpur,' I said. 'You go on, Terence.'

We were in the bicycle shed at the back of our school. Terence was the one who had called the meeting, so he was sitting on the grass-mower. I had written out the Emergency Meeting Notices and Cyril had gone around collecting everybody on his bicycle and giving them my notices to make sure they wouldn't forget. The trouble was that Cyril hadn't collected many people. There were only Harpur Brown and three of the fifth years and Scottie Watts and Harry Haxwell and Dribbler Wilson, though Cyril had told Dribbler he needn't come, because he was too small. Dribbler came in his football kit, just in case. Everybody else was at the swimming pool with Barnleck Youth Club. It was hard luck, but we had decided that the best thing was to go on with the meeting anyway.

'This meeting is about forming a football team to represent Red Row Primary School which we are all at,' Terence said. 'The team is to be called "Red Row Stars" and nicknamed "The Champs".'

'Why?' said Harpur. I think he was cross because the football team wasn't his idea. It wasn't Terence's idea either, it was mine.

'Because we *are* the Champs!' said Terence, and everybody cheered.

'First we have got to elect a Manager,' Terence went on. 'I call on the Honorary Secretary, Napper McCann, to accept nominations from the floor.'

It was the first time anyone had said I was Honorary Secretary.

'Why me?' I said.

'Because you wrote out all the notices,' said Terence.

'Oh,' I said. If it meant I had to write out notices all the time I didn't fancy it.

'Go on, Napper,' said Terence. 'This is too important to argue about everything. Call for nominations from the floor.'

'O K,' I said. 'I mean, I do. I call for nominations from the floor.' I didn't know what he meant, exactly, but Terence was right. Forming a football team was too important to argue about.

'I nominate the ceiling,' said Cyril, who thought he was being funny. 'I'm the floor, and I nominate the ceiling.'

'Shut up, Cyril,' said everyone.

'You ask everyone to say who they want to be Manager, Napper,' Terence explained. 'If somebody says somebody then somebody else has to second the somebody and if somebody else says somebody else and somebody else seconds it you have an election.'

'I see,' I said, though I was a bit lost with all the somebodys.

'I don't see,' said Cyril.

'That's 'cause you're stupid!' said Harry.

'Right,' Harpur said quickly, 'has anybody any suggestions about who should be our first manager?'

'I vote for T. Prince,' I said.

'I vote Napper McCann,' said Terence, at once.

We looked at each other.

'I don't want to be Manager,' I said. 'Anybody else?'

Nobody said anything.

'Who votes for Terence as Manager?' I said.

All the hands went up, except Terence's.

'You are Manager, Terence,' I said. 'Congratulations.'

'Player-Manager,' said Terence, firmly.

Nobody argued about that. Terence is one of the best players at Red Row. He is a great goalie, and he would be good on the field too if it wasn't for his asthma. He can't dash about because of his asthma so he has to stay in goal.

So Terence was elected to be the first Manager of Red Row Stars FC!

'What about Captain?' Harpur Brown said. 'I think I should be Captain.'

'I am the Manager, and I say who should be Captain,' said Terence, firmly. 'And I say ... I say Napper.'

'He can't be Captain and Honorary Secretary,' said Harpur.

'He's just resigned as Honorary Secretary,' said Terence. 'You've just been elected it!'

'Oh,' said Harpur. He didn't look pleased at being elected. He went and sat on his bike, looking as if he might ride off, but not doing it because he didn't want to miss anything.

'You're Captain, Napper,' Terence said.

'He can't be Captain,' Harry Haxwell said scornfully. 'He's only a P6! We can't have a kid for Captain, can we?'

'We wouldn't have a team if it wasn't for Napper,' Terence pointed out. 'It was his idea in the first place.'

'Harpur should be Captain,' Harry said.

'Napper *is* Captain,' said Terence. 'I'm Manager, and I say who is Captain. I say Napper because Napper is one of our best players, even if he is only a P6, and having the team was his idea.'

'I think Terence is right,' said Cyril.

'Let Napper be Captain, I don't mind,' said Harpur, sounding as if he *did* mind.

'Well I think Harpur should be it. Or me!' said Harry.

'Manager's decision is final!' said Cyril.

So I was made Captain. I'd much rather be Cap-

25

tain than Honorary Secretary any time, so I was pleased.

'Now,' said Terence. 'What about players? We'll have to have a first team pool.'

'Or puddle,' said Cyril.

'If you don't stop making jokes, Cyril, I'll punch you one,' said Harry Haxwell.

'You and who else?' said Cyril.

'Shut up, both of you!' said Terence, firmly.

'I've done a form,' I said. 'I did them on my Dad's typewriter. Everybody has to sign one, and signing makes them officially players for Red Row Stars FC.'

· RED ROW STARS FC
(THE CHAMPS).

This form signifies that I ....
of ....
.... am a properly signed and registered
player for the above named team. My age is ......
and I hereby certify that I am not a retained player
attached to any other football team.

Signed....................

Club Secretary....................

Date............

'Club Secretary,' said Harpur. 'Is that me, or is Honorary Secretary different?'

'Same,' said Terence. 'And Cyril can be Hon. Treasurer and buy the oranges for half-time.'

'It seems a bit silly to me,' said Harpur. 'We have a Player-Manager and a Captain and an Hon. Secretary and an Hon. Treasurer but we haven't got a team.'

'That is what this meeting is about,' said Terence. 'We've got to arrange about our team.'

'The Champs!' said Cyril, who was beginning to like the idea.

'The Champs, ha-ha-ha!' said a voice.

There was a terrible silence.

'Little Red Row Monkeys should be locked up in the zoo!' said the voice, and Hugh Cleland's big fat face came round the side of the shed. Bob Bridges was with him, and Gerry Cleland, Neil Collins and Knocker Lewis. They were all big for their age, and they thought they were the whole cheese.

'Monkeys!' said Hugh.

'Runny-nosed kids!' said Knocker, banging the big stick he was carrying against the corrugated tin of the shed. It made a noise like thunder, and Knocker did it again, hoping that one of us would take the stick from him, and then he could have a fight.

'Bet your team couldn't give us a match!' boasted Collins.

'I bet we could,' said Terence. 'We'd smash you to smithereens!'

'Come on, then, do it!' said Neil Collins, pulling his carroty hair out of his eyes. 'Five-a-side now, for the Football Champs of Barnleck title.'

'Right!' said Terence.

This is a picture of the Red Row Stars football five-a-side team who took the pitch for our first match, the battle for the Five-a-side Football Championship of Barnleck and District against our rivals, the Stringy Pants from St Gabriel's:

The players in the picture are: T. Prince, C. Small, H. Brown, H. Haxwell, N. McCann (Captain).

This is a picture of the Stringy Pants' five who were certain that they could beat us!

(L. to R.): G. Cleland   N. Collins   K. Lewis
H. Cleland   B. Bridges

3. The Five-a-side Title Match

When the teams lined up we realized that there had been nothing accidental about the Stringy Pants turning up at our meeting in the bicycle shed.

'All their best men, except Joe Fish!' grumbled Cyril. 'And all of them happened to be out for a walk across our school grounds, wearing their football kit!'

'We'll just have to beat their best men then, Cyril,' I said, and everybody cheered up.

Our goal was the bicycle shed and the other goal was a pile of coats and the elm tree. The pitch wasn't very big and it was bumpy, all of which favoured the Stringy Pants. They are a biff and bang football team who like to get in crunchy tackles, and the small pitch meant that there wouldn't be room for our players to nip away from them. The Stringy Pants play that way because they are usually up against teams who are smaller than they are, like the Cubs. But this time, because it was five-a-side, we were able to match them for size by playing our five biggest players. Their side was still bigger than our side, but not much, and we reckoned we had better players, so we thought we might win.

The teams lined up, and Red Row Stars kicked off, beginning our first ever competitive match.

Harpur Brown got the ball straight from the kick-off, and sent Bob Bridges the wrong way with a beautiful body swerve. Then he squared the ball to Red Row's Super Striker Napper McCann who hit it BOOM, hard and straight for the corner of the goal where Hugh Cleland dived full length and only just managed to reach it, turning it round the tree for a corner.

The whole Red Row Stars team except the goalie went up for the corner kick, and the whole Stringy Pants team lined up to mark us. That meant that with Harpur Brown, our schemer, taking the kick, the Stringy Pants had four of their men to deal with our three attackers. It looked hopeless!

But Harpur Brown had a clever tactical move up his sleeve, one that we had rehearsed in training. We didn't know that we would ever have a team when we were training, but we had been training just the same. Harpur had made up lots of schemes for free kicks and throw-ins, just in case we might ever need them.

Harpur took the ball and as he was placing it to take the corner kick he gave Terence Prince Secret Sign Number Four.

Terence Prince saw Harpur tapping his forehead ... which is Secret Sign Number Four ... and started to walk up the pitch from his goal. Terence isn't allowed to run, because of his asthma, but it was only a short pitch and Harpur intended taking advantage of it. It is the place we usually play, and there are tricks you can work in a small playground that wouldn't work on a full-size pitch. We all knew about Secret Sign Number Four, but the Stringy Pants didn't. The question was . . . would it work?

Harpur made as if to centre the ball from the corner, but instead he hit it back towards Terence, who was standing about twenty yards from the Stringy Pants' goal. Terence met the moving ball and hit it hard and high over the mass of players.

GOAL!

The ball bounced off the tree and whizzed into the back of the Stringy Pants' goal.

Terence had scored the first ever goal for Red Row Stars. It was a magnificent cracking hard shot from long range, resulting from Secret Plan Number Four, dreamed up by our schemer, Harpur Brown.

'Flukey!' grunted Hugh Cleland, who hadn't been able to see the ball because all his own players were standing in front of him, expecting the ball to be played into the goal-mouth. No one had paid any attention to Terence, until Harpur had struck the ball back to him and then BANG!

1–0 to Red Row Stars.

The Stringy Pants didn't like being one down. They all crowded up into attack, and Terence Prince had to make two terrific saves.

Then I got the ball and beat Knocker Lewis and shot WHAM like a rocket and the ball smashed past Hugh Cleland! It was a GREAT GOAL. Here is a picture of Napper McCann, Red Row Stars' Super Striker, scoring it:

The people bouncing about behind the goal are our fan club.

2–0 to Red Row Stars!

'Come on, Stars!' I shouted, running back to the centre. I had remembered that I was supposed to be Captain and encouraging everyone, though now that we were 2–0 up and coasting to Victory and the Five-a-side Championship of Barnleck we didn't need much encouraging.

We went on the attack again and Knocker Lewis kicked Harpur. After a lot of arguing we got a free kick and Super Striker Napper McCann took it and unleashed a powerful whizz-banger from twenty yards out which missed.

'You pass, next time,' Harpur said, trotting back to his position.

'I'm the Captain,' I said. 'I give the orders.'

'Oh yes?' said Harpur, who still wanted to be Captain himself. We were busy glaring at each other when the ball came out from Hugh Cleland in goal to Neil Collins who very cleverly nipped past Cyril and bore down on our goal. He hit a good shot and Terence got down to it, but the ball bounced away from him and Bob Bridges lashed it into the net!

2–1 to Red Row Stars! The match was wide open again!

I looked at Harpur, who shrugged. We both knew it was a goal that could have been stopped if we had

34

been paying attention to the game instead of fighting with each other.

Here is Bob Bridges scoring for the Stringy Pants and Cyril looking cross:

The Stringy Pants came straight back into the attack from the kick-off, hoping that they could snatch an equalizer. Terence was in action again, and dived at Bob Bridges's feet to save a certain goal. He threw the ball out to Cyril but the ball hit a bump and Cyril missed it and the next moment Neil Collins, the Stringy Pants' danger man, had fastened on to it. He darted past Cyril, who fell over his feet and landed on his bottom. Neil bore down on our goal with the ball under close control, and Harry Haxwell dashed after him. Just as Neil was going to shoot Harry banged into him, and Neil fell over.

'Penalty!' Knocker Lewis shouted, at the top of his voice.

'No it wasn't,' said Cyril.

'Yes it was!' said Knocker. 'I'll thump anybody who says it wasn't.'

I ran over and picked the ball up.

'Penalty,' I said. 'I'm the Captain, and I agree that it was a penalty. So stop arguing, Cyril.'

'Big head,' said Cyril, but I took no notice. Anyway, they had given us the free kick earlier.

'Twelve paces from the goal,' Harpur Brown said, and he began pacing them out. He placed the ball in position. It was up to Terence Prince to save Red Row Stars!

Neil Collins stopped rubbing the place where Harry Haxwell had banged him, and got ready to take the kick.

Neil is a clever player, even if he does play for St Gabriel's. He knew that if he could make Terence think that he was hitting the ball one way, and send the ball the other way instead, he would score . . . but he might be too smart, and miss altogether. If he hit the ball as hard as he could, without bothering too much about where it went, he would probably beat Terence for speed.

Terence crouched on his goal-line. He was thinking about the penalty too, and he used his brains.

I didn't understand what he was doing at first. I thought our Star goalie had gone mad in the middle of the Five-a-side Title match! There was our Star goalie, crouching down to save the penalty kick, but standing on the right-hand side of his goal, so that there was a big gap on the left.

'Terence!' I called.

Terence winked, and re-positioned himself slightly, but he still wasn't in the centre of his goal.

Neil would run up and shoot to Terence's left, and the Stringy Pants would be level.

I opened my mouth to shout a warning and Cyril said, 'Shut up, Napper! Can't you see what Terence is doing?'

And then I did see!

Terence had moved a little further to his right again, inviting Neil to shoot into the left-hand side of the net. He hoped that Neil would spot that he was in the wrong position. Here is a picture of Terence leaving space on the left-hand side of his goal:

At first Neil couldn't believe his eyes, and then I suppose he decided that Terence had made a mistake. The Stringy Pants all think that Terence is soft, because of his asthma and not being able to run, but everyone at Red Row knows that he is not.

Neil ran up and hit the ball as hard as he could towards the left-hand ... empty ... side of the goal, which was just where Terence wanted him to put it. As he struck the ball, Terence dived desperately in that direction. He can only have seen a flash of the ball whizzing towards the top corner of the net. Terence's outstretched fingers tipped the ball which spun upwards, struck the edge of the bicycle shed roof, and bounced down, where Terence grabbed it.

'Goal!' shouted Knocker Lewis.

'It wasn't!' I said. 'Terence caught it before it went over the line. It was the Super Save of the Season!'

'The ball hit the bar, and came down over the line,' Knocker said. 'Terence dragged it back.'

'I never,' said Terence, indignantly.

'Yes, you did,' said Hugh Cleland, who had come running up from his goal to argue. 'It was a brilliant goal. Your team gave away a dirty foul and Neil took a brilliant penalty and we got the goal we deserved, even though your goalie nearly got it.'

'No goal,' I said. Then I turned to Neil Collins. 'You took the penalty,' I said. 'What do you think?'

'I don't know,' said Neil, unhappily.

'Goal!' Knocker insisted.

'We could toss for it, or let Neil take another one,' I said.

'I don't see why we should,' Terence said. 'I'm sure I saved the first one.'

'I thought I had scored,' Neil said, very uncertainly.

'I don't think it was a goal,' I said. 'It was a brilliant save.'

'Goal,' said Knocker.

'Save!'

'Watch it, you cabbage-faced kid!' said Knocker.

'Who are you calling cabbage face?' I said, because I wasn't letting him get away with that, even if he was bigger than me. Knocker is bigger than almost anybody.

'You teach him manners, Knocker,' said Hugh Cleland.

Knocker pulled back his fist.

'STOP!'

A walking stick tapped Knocker sharply on the arm.

'What . . .' Knocker said, grabbing at it. Then . . . 'OUCH!' The walking stick rapped him on the knuckles, and Knocker bounced back, nursing his hand, with tears brimming in his eyes.

A small white-haired woman in a duffle coat stood her ground, right in the middle of the footballers. From the way she was waggling her walking stick, nobody was going to take any risks by going near her.

'Disgraceful!' she said.

'None of your business, missus!' muttered Hugh Cleland, beneath his breath.

'It is my business to stop bullies!' said the little woman. 'That is everybody's business, I should say.'

Knocker moved back, out of reach of her stick. He was still nursing his hand.

'That was a very fine save, young man,' said the little woman, turning to Terence. 'I saw every bit of it over the fence. The goalkeeper caught the ball after it bounced down from the crossbar. It did not cross the goal-line.'

'What crossbar?' muttered Knocker.

'Ref's decision is final,' said Harry, who was getting fed up with Knocker.

'What ref?' said Knocker.

They stood glaring at each other.

'I'm not going to play with these Red Row kids if they're going to go around inventing refs and crossbars!' snorted Hugh Cleland in a huff. 'Come on, St Gabriel's!'

'You're afraid of getting beaten,' Harpur Brown shouted as they started to go.

'We'll see you next Saturday on the proper football field, with a referee who isn't somebody's grannie!' said Hugh Cleland, very grandly, and the Stringy Pants stalked off the pitch and rode off down the school path on their bicycles.

'Hey!' said Dribbler Wilson. 'They've walked

off the field before the final whistle. That means we've won!'

There was a burst of wild cheering. Red Row Stars had won the very first match we had ever played.

'It is a good thing that that lady saw Terence's save, otherwise they'd never have given in,' Harpur said.

'We ought to thank her,' said Cyril.

But the woman in the duffle coat had gone.

After that, it was time for everyone to go home.

'Wait!' said Terence. 'What about the team? We haven't decided anything.'

'*We* don't have to,' said Scottie Watts, who was annoyed about being substitute and not in the team.

'Yes you do,' I said. 'There's jerseys, and a ball, and . . .'

'We're only the players,' said Scottie, with a grin. 'We leave that sort of thing to the Player-Manager!'

And off everybody went except Terence and Cyril Small and me and little Dribbler Wilson, who wasn't going to be much use because he was too small for organizing anything.

'What do we do?' Cyril said.

We picked up our coats and went back to the bicycle shed, talking about it.

'Tell you what,' Terence said. 'I don't really mind if they leave everything to us. We will manage it all right. And . . . And WE WON, didn't we?'

2–1 to Red Row Stars! We were the Five-a-side

Champions of Barnleck after our very first ever match, because the Stringy Pants had walked off the field before the final whistle.

'All that we've got to do now,' said Cyril, 'is to beat them in the proper match, next Saturday!'

4. How We Got Organized

Mr Hope is the Headmaster of Red Row Primary School. The next thing we had to do was to persuade him that we ought to have a football team.

'You're the Manager, Terence,' Cyril said. 'You do the talking.'

'I don't like this,' Terence said. 'I get all the dirty work.'

We were standing outside Mr Hope's room, waiting for him to come in. It was Monday morning, and we only had five days to get organized.

'And have a practice match,' Cyril reminded us. 'We'll have to have a practice match before we meet the Stringy Pants. We need a chance to work at our tactics.'

'One thing at a time,' Terence said. 'First Mr Hope.'

Mr Hope came in.

'Sir! Sir!' said Terence, stepping forward.

'Good morning! Good morning! Good morning!' he said, and rushed straight past us, closing the door of his office behind him with a bang.

'Sir . . .' Terence said to the door, but the door was still shaking from the way Mr Hope had slammed it, and it didn't reply.

'Knock,' I said doubtfully.

'He looked in a hurry,' Cyril said, beginning to back away down the hall. 'Maybe we should come back later.'

'We've got to fix things up this morning,' Terence said firmly. 'You knock, Napper.'

'OK,' I said, not very happily. 'I'll do the knocking, but you do the talking. That is the final decision of the Committee, isn't it, Cyril?'

'Agreed,' said Cyril, who didn't mind who did the talking and knocking so long as it wasn't C. Small.

'It isn't agreed,' said Terence. 'Harpur is the Hon. Secretary. He must be on the Committee and he isn't here, so the Committee can't agree anything.'

'Harpur wanted to be Captain,' Cyril said. 'You should have made him Captain. Then he would have been more use.'

'I don't mind if he is Captain, if he wants to be,' I said. I did mind really. I like being Captain, but we needed everybody helping if we were going to get our football team. I would rather have a football team and not be Captain, than be a Captain with no team.

'I mind,' said Terence. 'Harpur is too big for his football boots, sometimes. I am the Manager, and I decide who is Captain.'

'And you do the talking,' said Cyril, as I knocked on Mr Hope's door.

'Come in! Come in! Come in!' Mr Hope called.

We went in. He was sitting at his desk chewing a pencil and telephoning at the same time.

'Two, two, two,' he said to the telephone. 'Good morning! Good morning! Good morning! Sorry! I've already Goodmorninged you three, haven't I? Apologize. Very busy! What do you want?'

'Please Sir, we want to start a football team,' Terence said.

'Hullo, hullo, hullo!' Mr Hope was speaking into the telephone. 'Hope here. Red Row. Good morning, good morning, good morning! Mr Laker please. Laker.' He cupped his hand over the receiver. 'Football team?' he said. 'Good idea!'

'We want to start one.' Terence said. 'We've already started it really. It is called Red Row Stars and we played . . .'

'Hullo, hullo, hullo. Laker? A moment, a moment, a moment, please.' He turned back to us. 'Team . . . team . . . team . . . See Miss Fellows.'

'Thank you, sir,' Terence said.

'Laker, Laker, Laker . . . that you?' he was bellowing down the telephone as we trooped out into the passage.

'Does that mean we can have our team?' I asked doubtfully.

'He didn't *exactly* say "yes",' said Cyril.

'And he didn't say "no",' said Terence. 'And that means we can have our team!'

'Have team! Have team! Have team!' I said,

doing my famous Mr Hope imitation, and then stopping quickly, in case he heard me. Mr Hope wastes a lot of time saying everything three times, but he seems to hear three times as well as anybody else too.

We went to see Miss Fellows.

'Football team?' said Miss Fellows, wearily. 'You kids!'

'Mr Hope said, said, said,' said Terence, unable to get out of the habit, and finding it useful for once, because he didn't want to say exactly what Mr Hope had said, in case Miss Fellows disagreed about it meaning '*Yes, you can have your team*' and thought it meant '*No, you can't possibly*' instead.

'I don't know who is going to organize it,' she said. 'I agree, it is a smashing idea. But there are only four of us to manage all the school activities, you know. We have our hands full with you lot already.'

'Please, Miss, we'll organize it ourselves, Miss,' said Terence quickly.

'Well . . .' said Miss Fellows, doubtfully. She has funny frizzy hair and we call her Baboon. I don't think baboons have funny frizzy hair but we call her Baboon anyway. She isn't bad.

'We have a real match arranged for Saturday,' I said, proudly. 'We're playing St Gabriel's.'

Miss Fellows's eyes almost popped out of her glasses!

'Are you indeed?' she said. 'You've spoken to Mr Thompson, of course?'

Mr Thompson is the Headmaster of St Gabriel's.

'Well, no,' I said. 'Not exactly, Miss. We thought you would speak to him. The Stringy Pants challenged us, Miss. That's why we've got to have a team. We are playing them on Saturday and we've got to have a proper official team or we can't play them properly, can we? We didn't think about Mr Thompson, though.'

'And you want me to speak to Mr Thompson,' she said. 'So much for organizing it all yourselves.' She stopped talking and looked at us. 'You want to have a team,' she said. 'But what about players? This isn't a very big school, you know. St Gabriel's have dozens to pick from.'

'We've got enough, Miss. We've worked it all out at our emergency meeting, Miss.' We hadn't really, but we thought if we made it sound all worked out she would let us have our team, and we could work it out afterwards.

'Well . . . you can use one of the school balls, I suppose. What about a pitch?'

'The Rec., Miss. All the teams in the Junior League use the Rec.'

'And you could change here, I suppose. Though I'll have to speak to the Caretaker. Bang goes my Saturday morning, though!' She looked rueful at that, and for a moment I thought she was going to decide we couldn't have our team, because it would muck up her shopping or whatever she did on Saturday mornings.

'We've *got* to have a team, Miss,' I said, desperately. 'The Stringy Pants are calling us names.'

'Are they indeed?' she said, with a laugh, and I knew we had won. 'Let me see . . . what about jerseys?'

'School shirts, Miss,' said Terence. 'We've all got grey shirts, because that's the uniform. We're going to get as many old ones as we can, and put numbers on the back . . . you can cut them out of plastic, and stick them. Then we'll be a proper team. Red Row Stars!'

'Grey shirts, red numbers, black shorts . . . we'll use our gym shorts . . . and grey socks.'

'I've never heard of a team playing in grey before,' she said.

'It'll give us an advantage, Miss,' Terence explained. 'We won't have to change our jerseys if there is a colour clash, because there won't be one. If nobody else is in grey there can't be, can there?'

'Well, Terence, you seem to have thought of everything, don't you? You've done so much thinking that I can't really let you down. I'll speak to Mr Thompson for you, and see if we can fix up your precious match. When you've played St Gabriel's, we'll have another think about whether this school is really big enough to have a team. If you expect me to give up every Saturday morning for you, you've got to show me you are worth it!'

We went off to tell the others.

'You can call your team The Baboon's Babies,' Ugly Irma said.

'You'll laugh on the other side of your face when we beat St Gabriel's,' Terence said.

'Which side do you mean?' asked Cyril, looking at her. 'The side that looks like an elephant, or the side that looks like a hippo?'

Then Irma hit him with her school-bag and Cyril pulled her hair and my sister Avril poured her orange juice into Cyril's gym shoes.

'Now you're all wet, like your team,' she said.

Miss Fellows looked into our room, after break.

'Eleven o'clock, Saturday morning,' she said. 'Mr Hogan will open up the hall for you to change in. All right?'

'Great, Miss!' said Terence.

'Our first match!' said Cyril, sounding slightly awed. I don't think he really believed we could do it.

'All players report to the bicycle shed at lunchtime,' our Manager Terence Prince announced. 'I want a full-scale turnout for practice.'

'I won't be able to come, Terence,' said Harpur.

'People who don't practise, don't play,' said Terence firmly.

Then Harpur went up to Terence and said something that the rest of us couldn't hear.

'Oh!' said Terence. 'GREAT!'

'Keep it under your hat,' said Harpur.

'Right,' said Terence. 'All meet at the bicycle shed except the Honorary Secretary, who is hereby excused practice on important team business.'

Harpur came rushing back into school just as we were finishing our practice game.

He jumped off his bicycle and dumped it in the shed. Then he came running across to us.

'It's fixed!' he said.

'What's fixed?'

'Practice Match,' Harpur said, importantly. 'I am the Hon. Secretary and I haven't been doing anything and everybody else has. So now I've done something! I've fixed a match with Maypoleleaf Cubs on the Rec. Tuesday night! I've spoken to their Akela and Miss Fellows. The Match is on!'

5. Stars Versus Maypoleleaf Cubs

This is a drawing of the Red Row Stars team that lined up for the practice match against Maypoleleaf Cubs on the Rec. field:

Top row (L. to R.): Scottie Watts   Scuddy Rodgers
Peter Scott   Cyril Small   Duncan Forbes   John Deacon
Mark Bellow (substitute)
Bottom row: Joe Small   Terence Prince
Napper McCann (captain)   Harpur Brown   Harry Haxwell

Dribbler Wilson from the fourth year was our official trainer because he turned up, as usual, with his kit and boots and wanted to do something.

You will see from the picture of our team what our problem was. It was Joe Small, who is Cyril's little brother, Scuddy Rodgers, and Duncan Forbes. They are small. They were smaller than the smallest cubs who had played against the Stringy Pants the previous Saturday. Mark Bellow is bigger . . . a bit bigger . . . but he is no good at football, and he didn't want to play. Daniel Rooney is in our year and is very big and plays sometimes, but he was off with measles. So there we were. We had the Five Super Stars, the same Five who had brought the first ever Five-a-side Championship of Barnleck to Red Row by defeating the Stringy Pants 2–1 in the Grand Final in our playground. Then we had the three little ones. That made eight. The last three, John Deacon, Scottie Watts and Peter Scott, were big enough, but they played football like statues. We decided to put the big but no good ones in defence where they could bump into the Cubs even if they couldn't catch them and the little ones in attack with Harpur Brown and me, where they might do some good by laying off the ball for us to run on to. We played 4–2–4, and this was our line up:

T. Prince

P. Scott   C. Small   H. Haxwell   S. Watts

J. Deacon   H. Brown

S. Rodgers   N. McCann (capt.)   D. Forbes   J. Small

The big idea was that Harpur would lay the ball

forward to the little ones and follow up himself and I would go for goal at every opportunity, leaving Cyril and Harry Haxwell to tidy up behind us, and letting big Deacon and Scott and Watts lumber around the defence collecting the Cubs who bounced off Cyril and Harry. If Cyril and Harry could button up the middle of the defence and Harpur could lay the ball forward I would be bound to do something, especially with the titchy Cubs' goalie. I spent most of Monday evening practising lobbing the ball up where he couldn't get it! And most of Monday night dreaming about the goals I was going to get!

By the time we were dressed in our World Famous grey shirts with red numbers we were convinced we were in for a big win, just the thing to set us up for the key match on Saturday against our deadly enemies from St Gabriel's.

'Everybody ready?' I said.

Everybody was.

Miss Fellows handed me the ball, and we trotted out of the hall and down to the pitch, keeping in a straight line just like England at Wembley. Dribbler Wilson and Miss Fellows came behind us, carrying the sponge and the first-aid kit. They should have been carrying the oranges but Cyril had forgotten about getting them, so we had no oranges for our first match on the Rec. pitch, which is the pitch all the proper Junior League teams play on in Barnleck.

When we saw the Cubs we got a shock.

They were kicking in at the High Road end, dressed in their usual red shirts and white shorts.

Cyril was the first one to spot it. He stopped and gaped, then he tore up the line to me, forgetting all about keeping his place so that we would look like England.

'They're big!' he gasped. 'They've got lots more big ones than they had on Saturday!'

'They can't have,' said Terence. 'Even Cubs don't grow that quickly!'

But they had. The Cubs on the pitch were great big enormous ones, bigger than anybody on our side except Harry Haxwell.

'We can't play them,' Cyril said, in a small voice. That's a joke really. Small voice. Cyril Small. It didn't seem much of a joke at the time.

Then their Akela came up and said hello to Miss Fellows and what a nice evening it was for the boys to be out and then she said. 'I hope your team don't mind, dear, but I've drafted in one or two of our Scouts, so that we can make a match of it!'

'Oh, never worry,' said Miss Fellows. 'We don't mind at all. It is all a bit of fun, isn't it?'

'They take it very seriously, you know!' said the Akela. 'Our boys were badly beaten on Saturday by those bigger boys from St Gabriel's. If I hadn't let them play one or two of the Scouts, I'd have had a strike on my hands.'

They both laughed at this.

Red Row Stars weren't laughing.

'*One or two of our Scouts*' was really five, and Colin Thomas who had had the flu when they played St Gabriel's was back. That meant that only four of the Cub players who had turned out against the Stringy Pants were on their team against us. Worst of all they had put one of their Scouts in goal, and their little goalie was playing out on the field. We had seen enough of his quick-thinking to know that he would give us trouble, and it meant that all the practice Harpur and I had been putting in on high balls was wasted. We had spent most of Monday evening lobbing high balls in above Dribbler Wilson expecting that we would be able to do the same thing to the Cubs' goalie, and now they had a big one with a track suit and red and yellow gloves and knee and elbow pads. He was jumping around doing exercises and flicking the ball over the bar and giving instructions to his defenders about being in command of his area. We would be lucky to get a single shot past him!

'It isn't fair,' Cyril muttered.

'They'll give us a hard match, anyway,' said Terence. 'It will be great training for Saturday.'

Well, it was, and it wasn't!

We were playing twenty-five minutes each way.

The Maypoleleaf Cubs' Akela was refereeing the first half, and Miss Fellows was to referee the second. The Akela blew her whistle and the Cubs kicked off.

Straight down the field ran the two biggest Scouts: One. Two. BANG!

55

1–0 to Maypoleleaf Cubs.

Five minutes later it was 2–0, when the little goalie who had come out on the field ran a ring round Harry Haxwell and put the centre-forward clear.

Then 3–0, when Terence turned a cross into his own net instead of putting it over the bar.

'Some goalie!' grumbled Harpur, but it wasn't Terence's fault, because one of the Scouts was pulling his goalie jersey, only the Akela didn't see.

3–0, and there were still ten minutes to go to half time!

'Come on, Red Row Stars!' Miss Fellows shouted cheerfully from the touchline, but how could we come on? The three biggest Scouts and the little ex-goalie were almost playing us on their own. Everytime the big Scouts got the ball they would bang it forward and run like hares, not really playing football at all, but beating our defenders because their legs were so long.

They got another goal. 4–0 to Maypoleleaf.

'It is no use, Harpur,' I said. 'I am going back into defence. You take one of them, I'll take one of them, and Cyril and Harry Haxwell can take the third one. If we just follow the three biggest around we may be able to stop them scoring any more.'

I ran back to the defence, and immediately the big Scouts came at us again. Terence was diving and punching and making Super Saves and everybody was trying very hard at the back, except Harry

Haxwell. He had started arguing with Terence about the own goal Terence had given away. It was a very silly thing to do considering all the saves Terence had made, but it was typical Harry.

'Come on, Harry,' I said. 'Tackle.'

The cub who had been their goalie the last time came at Harry, showed him the ball, switched it inside and glided past him. Harry came rushing after him. The Cub stopped dead and stood on the ball. Harry skidded past him, and fell over.

'Haxwell the Hacker!' somebody roared from the touchline, and I recognized Knocker Lewis's voice. That was all we needed. 4–0 down, and the Stringy Pants on the touchline cheering on the Cubs!

The Cub passed to the big Scout I was marking. I gave him room on the outside, and he moved there, thinking he could go round me, but really I was letting Cyril get back to cover. I delayed the tackle until he had worked out towards the corner flag, then I put in a slide tackle. The ball ran loose and John Deacon put it behind for a corner.

'Don't jump in at people, Harry,' I said, as we lined up. 'You are losing your temper.'

'Dry up, Napper,' he said.

The corner came over and Terence rose like a bird and caught it, even though the two big Scouts in the middle were crowding him again. I thought the Akela would give us a free kick for barging the goalie, but she didn't. Terence saw me moving clear of the Scout I had been marking at the edge of the area and he threw me a short ball, so that I could take it in my stride. I switched inside and drove the ball across to Joe Small, who is smart even if he is small. Joe didn't stop the ball at all. He tapped it back to Scottie Watts who was coming rushing up behind him to over-lap. Scottie got the ball, checked, and then swung the ball across the goal towards the Cubs' far post where Harpur Brown put in a flying header that smacked against the post and came bouncing out. John Deacon came steaming up to slash it into the net. He drew his foot back and smashed the ball but he missed the goal altogether!

This is what we did, leading up to the moment when John Deacon missed a certain goal:

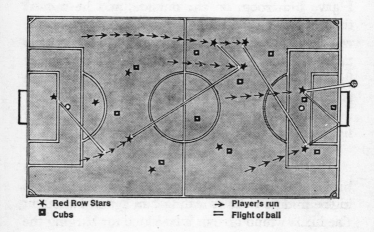

✷ Red Row Stars	→ Player's run
◘ Cubs	= Flight of ball

58

'Yo-ho! Red Row are Rubbish!' sang out the Stringy Pants players who were lining the touchline.

The big Scout I had been marking got the ball but I put in a magnificent Napper McCann special tackle, which was great only I missed him. He ran on towards our goal and smacked the ball hard. Terence made a cat leap to one side of the goal and got a hand to it. The ball spun up in the air and struck the underside of the bar and bounced down into our net.

5–0 to Maypoleleaf Cubs, and it still wasn't half time.

'We want Six!' chanted the Stringy Pants on the touchline.

'That was your man who scored that one,' Harry said to me, as we lined up again. 'You can't blame me for that one!'

'Wise up, Harry,' said Harpur, and off we went again.

Half time.

5–0 to Maypoleleaf Cubs!

> *'Five–Four–Three–Two–One.*
> *Give the Cubs Another One!'*

That was what the Stringy Pants were chanting. 'Easy. E–A–S–Y!' Knocker Lewis shouted, right in Miss Fellows' ear, but he pushed off when she turned round to see who had done it.

'You're doing your best, boys, hard luck,' said Miss Fellows.

We didn't say anything. We were choked.

During half time the Stringy Pants moved round behind Terence's goal. When the game restarted they began chanting: 'Easy! Easy!' and 'One–Two–Three–Four–Five. Cubs will eat the kids alive.' By the kids they meant us. They started shouting that Miss Fellows should change our nappies.

'Come on,' said Cyril gritting his teeth. 'We'll show them.'

But we didn't.

They got three more goals in the second half, and they could have had more if their Akela hadn't taken two of the Scouts off, to even things up. The goals weren't really our fault, except for the last one. It was Harry Haxwell who caused it, and as usual he did it by losing his temper when somebody had beaten him.

'Penalty!' said Miss Fellows, sternly, picking up the little Cub whom Harry had flattened on the edge of the goal area.

Bang!

In it whizzed, despite Terence's desperate dive.

'That was your fault, Harry!' Terence grumbled, picking the ball out of the back of the net.

'Oh yes?' said Harry. 'I suppose you blame me for all the silly goals you have let in, as usual?'

'No,' said Terence. 'I blame you for that one

though. You had no need to trip him. You should learn to play football properly instead of knocking people over.'

'Oh, should I?' said Harry. 'That's all right then. If you think I can't play football, I won't.'

And he walked off the pitch, pulling his shirt off as he went.

'Hey, Harry!' I shouted, but Harry paid no attention.

'Let him go, Napper,' said Cyril. 'We'll bring on our substitute.'

Mark Bellow came on, but he might as well have stayed off. He wandered round the field looking at things, instead of playing football.

Three minutes to go. 8–0.

'We can't win it now,' Harpur said.

It was a silly thing to say. The Stringy Pants players on the line were saying it all for us. They were dancing around behind Terence's goal and really enjoying themselves making jokes at our expense.

'We can get one goal, at least.' I said. 'We must get one goal, just to shut Knocker and his friends up.'

'Right,' said Harpur. 'We've lost the game. Forget about defence. We'll go forward and attack them.'

So the next time he got the ball Harpur set off on his own on a weaving run. He went past three of them and squared the ball to me. I played a wall pass behind the centre-half and Harpur ran on, taking the ball in his stride. He smacked the ball hard at goal and the goalie plunged sideways and knocked the ball up into the air.

I was running in at full speed and I saw it spinning up in front of me. Too far in front, I couldn't reach it! So I took off in a full-length super dive and smacked the ball with my forehead high up into the top corner of the net.

GOAL!

Everybody went wild!

Red Row Stars had scored their first Star Goal, a brilliant header by Super Striker Napper McCann in the closing minutes of the game.

Here is a picture of me scoring our goal:

I lay on my back in the net, arms outstretched, and Harpur ran in and lifted me out. We were all dancing about as though we had won the game, instead of losing it by seven clear goals.

The final whistle went before the Cubs had time to kick off.

It was a Super Stupendous Star Goal, but it was the only one we got.

8–1 to Maypoleleaf Cubs.

We trudged back up the lane to school.

'8–1!' Terence groaned.

'We were terrible,' I said.

'Awful,' said Harpur.

But it was Cyril who said what we had all been thinking, without anyone else having dared to say it.

'If the Cubs beat us 8–1, how many will the Stringy Pants beat us by on Saturday?'

There was a gloomy silence.

'They beat the Cubs 4–1,' I said. 'And the Cubs beat us.'

'I always said it was a stupid idea,' said Cyril. 'We haven't got enough good players to make a team.'

'I suppose we could call off the game,' said Terence, sitting down on the school steps to take his boots off.

'If Miss Fellows doesn't make us call it off,' said Cyril. 'You know she said she didn't want to miss

63

her Saturday morning shopping for nothing. And that's what we are, nothing.'

'We can't call it off,' I said. 'Knocker would never let us forget it.'

Everyone agreed with that.

'There's only one thing we can do, now,' I said. 'We've got to play that game against the Stringy Pants on Saturday, and we've got to go out and win it!'

Miss Fellows came bustling up. 'Put your jerseys in Mr Hogan's hamper, boys,' she said. 'I've arranged for them to be washed. And Terence . . . you're the Manager, aren't you? I want to see you and Napper and the rest of the bigger boys in your room at break tomorrow. There's some hard talking to be done!'

Then off she went.

'What's that about?' Cyril asked.

'She's going to tell us that she can't be bothered with a team that loses 8–1,' said Harpur, dismally. 'I'm afraid that this is the end of Red Row Stars!'

'Yo ho!' shouted Avril, when I got home. 'Was 'ums playing fooball den, icle brudder?'

'Shut up,' I said.

'Ya! 8–1!' Avril said.

'It's bad enough without you going on about it,' I said.

'Dere, dere, den,' said Avril. 'Ums stupid icle fooball team got beated, did id?'

She went on and on for hours.

6. Team Talks

We all gathered in the P6 and P7 room at break-time, waiting for Miss Fellows. She came in a bit late, clutching her cup of coffee and looking at her watch.

'Sorry I'm late, boys,' she said. 'But now, let's get on with it, shall we?'

'Miss, Miss, please, Miss!' said Terence, putting up his hand. We had all decided that Terence would do the talking for us, and try to persuade Miss Fellows to let us have our team, at least until Saturday, so that we could play the Stringy Pants. If they beat us by a bag full of goals it would be awful, but not as awful as if we didn't turn up to play them. Then they would say we were kids who needed our nappies changed and couldn't even raise a football team.

'Yes, Terence?' said Miss Fellows.

'Please, Miss, the boys asked me to say we're sorry about wasting your time and not playing well and letting in eight goals and making the School look silly, not even beating the Cubs whom everybody beats . . .'

'The Cubs and the Scouts,' put in Miss Fellows.

'They played some much bigger boys against you, Terence.'

'I know, Miss. But still, Miss . . . 8–1!'

'We were rubbish!' said Cyril, looking very down in the mouth.

'I thought you all tried very hard,' said Miss Fellows. 'You were up against a very big team and they over-ran you. But, with one exception, none of you has anything to be ashamed of.'

We were all a bit puzzled. She didn't seem to be mad at us at all.

'I'm not worried about our team losing the game,' she said. 'But I am worried about one thing that happened.'

She stopped, and tapped her pencil against the desk.

'Harry Haxwell?' she said.

Harry stood up.

'Harry Haxwell! I could scarcely believe my eyes when I saw you walking off the field! In the middle of the game too! And when your team was getting badly beaten! What have you to say for yourself?'

Harry had gone red all over his face. He stood at his desk and shuffled his feet, looking for an answer. Then he said. 'It was them, Miss. Napper and Terence. They were getting at me, Miss!'

'That is no excuse, Harry,' she said. 'No excuse at all. I hardly know what to say to you. Except this . . . now you have walked off, you won't find it so easy to walk on again, not if I have any say in the matter.'

Harry gaped at her. 'Miss?' he said.

'You've got to learn, Harry. It is an honour to be picked for any team. Well, by walking off you indicated that you didn't want to play with the others. I don't see how you can expect to be picked for the team next time, Harry, do you?'

'It's St Gabriel's, Miss,' Harry said.

'I don't care if it is Manchester United,' said Miss Fellows.

Terence put up his hand.

'Miss? Miss?'

'Yes, Terence?'

'Miss, it's St Gabriel's. They're all big. Harry is big. We need Harry, Miss, or we just won't have a chance.'

'If you need him so much, maybe you shouldn't have shouted at him on the pitch,' said Miss Fellows, sternly. 'Harry is quite right, you know. He is rather a clumsy player, but you and Napper do single people out for criticism on the field.'

'I'm the Captain, Miss. I'm supposed to do that,' I said.

'If your way of doing it is to go round the field shouting criticisms at people, then you might be better not being Captain,' she said.

'Harpur Brown should be Captain,' Scottie Watts said.

'I don't want to be Captain,' Harpur said quickly.

'I think Napper is a good skipper and I stick by him!'

I gave him a big grin. It was very good of him, because I knew he really wanted to be Captain, and he was saying that he didn't to stick up for me.

'I don't think we should get involved with changing Captains at this stage,' said Miss Fellows. 'But certainly I think you all have a lesson to learn about being a team. Don't stand there and shout at each other. If you see somebody making a mistake, double back and try to cover up for him. And if you can't cover up, and somebody gives a goal away . . . like your Manager, Terence, punching the ball into his own net for the third goal . . . forget it! The player who has made the mistake is feeling worse about it than you are! And the more mistakes he makes, the worse he will feel, and he'll make more and more mistakes if people keep shouting at him and telling him what to do. By all means talk to each other on the pitch and try to point out things that are going wrong . . . but on Tuesday you almost ended up fighting each other. That is not good for you or for your team, and certainly not good for this school. If I see it happening again, I will have to reconsider whether you can go on having an official school team.'

'You mean we can?' said Terence. 'You won't call off our match on Saturday?'

'Of course not,' said Miss Fellows. 'What an idea! You've all seen what can happen to a player who loses his temper on the field, and you've seen how other people shouting at him can make it worse. I hope you'll learn from it. No. The match on Saturday is on! After that last display, I don't know how you're going to do it, but I hope you win!'

And off she went.

'What about Harry?' I said, when she had gone. 'Does that mean he can't play against St Gabriel's?'

'It isn't fair,' said Harry. 'It wasn't my fault. It was you and Terence!'

'Partly it was,' said Terence. 'But you did have something to do with it, Harry. And you walked off after all. We didn't.'

'I don't know if I want to play any more,' said Harry. 'It's a rotten team, anyway.'

'Is that so, Harry?' said Terence, with a cold edge to his voice.

'You and Napper and Harpur want it all your own way,' said Harry.

'We only started the team, that's all!' I said. 'All you've done is cause rows.'

'OK, Big Head. I don't care. I'm not playing for your rotten team ever again!' said Harry.

The Hon. Treasurer, Cyril Small, brought a note round to my house at tea-time.

RED ROW STARS FC
Special Meeting of Selection Committee
Bicycle Shed 3 p.m.
Signed C. SMALL
(HON. TREAS.)

'You could have told me that, Cyril,' I said.

'I know,' he said. 'But I didn't. Now give it back to me so that I can show it to everybody else on the Committee!'

I gave it back to him. Sometimes I think Cyril Small is a bit nuts.

'It doesn't say what day the meeting is, Cyril!' I pointed out.

'Tomorrow, stupid,' he said.

We got most of the names filled in very quickly.

'Just because the system didn't work the first time it doesn't mean that it will never work,' Terence said. 'Anyway, we have to deal with the little players and the big ones who can't play, and I'm sure that this is the best way to arrange them.' So we wrote out the team list for the fixture against the Stringy Pants from St Gabriel's.

T. Prince

P. Scott	C. Small	———	S. Watts
	J. Deacon	H. Brown	
S. Rodgers	N. McCann	D. Forbes	J. Small

That left a gap in the centre of the defence, where Harry Haxwell should have been if he hadn't decided that he was too good to play for us.

'Mark Bellow,' said Terence, doubtfully.

I looked at Cyril and Harpur. Together with Terence, we had elected ourselves as the Selection Committee, because we were all that were left of the

Super Stars of Red Row who had won the Five-a-side Championship of Barnleck.

'You can't leave me with Mark in the middle of the defence,' said Cyril. 'I'd have to run myself rotten covering for him.'

'Well,' said Terence. 'We could move Scottie into the middle to cover you, and stick Mark out on the flank. At least he is big.'

'We need Scottie to mark Neil Collins,' I said. 'I mean, Neil is too good for Scottie, but at least Scottie will make a match of it. If we put Mark out there to take him, Collins will rip us apart down that side. Then you and Scottie will have to go across to cover and that will let Gerry Cleland and Bob Bridges loose in the middle.'

'Maybe Harry would still play, if we asked him,' Harpur said. 'We could try, couldn't we? Otherwise we won't have a defence.'

Terence shook his head. 'Miss Fellows says he is suspended for one game, because of walking off. Even if he wanted to play, she won't let him. And he doesn't want to play, at least he says he doesn't. No. Forget about Harry. I think I know what we'll do, anyway.'

He took the team sheet and ran his pencil through Harpur's name.

We all gaped at him.

'Hey,' said Harpur. 'That's me you've just crossed out!'

'I'm not dropping you,' said Terence. 'I'm just

moving you back. The Stringy Pants are so strong up front that we have to have cover. So, your name goes in where Harry would have been. That means that you and Cyril can cover Bob Bridges and Gerry Cleland between you, with Scottie doing his best to keep Neil Collins out on the wing.'

'Oh,' said Harpur.

'Great,' said Cyril. 'I think that that makes a lot of sense.'

'Yes,' I said. 'But.'

'But what, Napper?'

'If you take Harpur away from mid-field and put him at the back, who is going to lay the ball on for me? You saw what happened when I came back against the Cubs. There was no one left up front to do any attacking, and Harpur and I had to make long runs from defence.'

'You got a goal,' Cyril pointed out.

'They got eight,' I said. 'I can see that Cyril has a problem at the back, but I need someone in the middle who can hold the ball and lay it off.'

'If we had someone who could do that, I could come forward a bit now and then and help Napper,' Harpur said. 'But I can't be in all places at once.'

'Joe Small lays the ball off well,' I said. 'But he is no good at holding it.'

'Napper could lie back in my old position,' said Harpur. 'We could move Joe into the centre spot.'

'Napper is our Super Striker,' said Terence. 'You know we rely on him for goals. He leads the attack. He'll have to go for goal every time he gets the chance, and he may not get much help because Harpur will have to stay deep most of the time.'

'All right,' said Cyril. 'Harpur and I button down the middle of the defence. You do miracles in goal, Terence. Napper goes poaching for goal any time we can get a ball forward to him. But who runs the middle of the field?'

Terence picked up his pencil, and wrote a name on the team sheet, where he had crossed Harpur's out.

It was little Dribbler Wilson's!

7. The Big Match

This was our team for the Big Match with St Gabriel's Primary (The Stringy Pants) on Barnleck Recreation Ground, which was the game we had all been waiting for:

T. Prince

P. Scott   C. Small   H. Brown   S. Watts

J. Deacon   D. Wilson

S. Rodgers   N. McCann (capt.)   D. Forbes   J. Small

Substitute M. Bellow

Travelling Official Miss E. Fellows

It was the best team we could put out, although we were certainly going to miss Harry Haxwell.

We changed in the school hall, and Miss Fellows took a photograph of us for the school board before we trotted down to the Rec. pitch.

The pitch was in good condition, clearly marked, and somebody from the Council had put on a new set of nets. I don't suppose they knew it was a special Challenge Match, but maybe they did. We were first out.

'I expect they think they'll make us nervous, standing about waiting for them,' Terence said to

75

Miss Fellows, but she only laughed and told him not to be silly.

It didn't need that to make us nervous.

We all had butterflies inside . . . at least I did, I know that, and even Terence was looking pale. It was the Big Match, the one we had to do well in.

The most nervous of the lot was Dribbler Wilson! I went across to him, to see if I could cheer him up.

'Well, Dribbler, fit?' I said.

'Um-um!' he gulped.

'Listen, Dribbler,' I said. 'You are the youngest player on the pitch, and all the Stringy Pants are going to think you are on the field to make up the number. But you're not. Terence has selected you to play because he believes you can do a job for us in the middle of the field. We all know you can dribble round anyone, even if you are small. What we don't know is whether you'll be able to stand up to the tackling. The Stringy Pants will be out to shake you early on. You must stand up to them! Give as good as you get! And don't be afraid of people like Knocker Lewis. You are a better foot-baller than Knocker any day.'

Dribbler nodded his head unhappily.

'Yes you are!' I insisted. 'You know you are. And Harpur will try to come from behind to help you. I'll be making runs all the time, trying to find a space. Use your dribbling to draw them on to you, then look for me and release the ball. If I can slip Joe

Fish in the middle I'm sure I can smack a few in.'

'I'll try, Napper,' he said, and he went away to tie his laces again.

'I hope he is going to be all right,' I said to John Deacon. 'Listen John, you'll have to do a lot of the work Harpur does, because Harpur will be at the back, and Dribbler probably isn't up to taking on the big lads.'

'All right, Skipper,' John said, and he rolled up his sleeves. I knew John would do his best.

'Ready, Harpur?' I said.

Harpur nodded. He didn't say anything. He knew what he had to do.

The Stringy Pants team came running down the hill from their school, and it was then we got our first surprise. It wasn't just the team we were up against! They had brought half their school with them! There seemed to be people in St Gabriel's uniforms everywhere, laughing and joking and milling round their players as they came out on to the field. I looked round for our supporters.

Miss Fellows. Three of the fourth years come to cheer Dribbler. Mark Bellow, who wasn't really a supporter . . . and somebody else, standing down by the swings, away from everybody else.

'Harry's come,' I said to Terence.

'I wish he was playing,' Terence said, and I knew he was regretting the row that had led to Harry being out of the team.

Mr Thompson, the Head of St Gabriel's, came

across the pitch to where Miss Fellows was standing.

'We seem to have thought of everything, except the referee,' he said. 'Would you have any objection to my taking the whistle?'

Miss Fellows said she hadn't.

'I don't like that,' Cyril grumbled, but there was no time to fuss about it, for Mr Thompson took a whistle from his pocket and blew it. It was time for me to go to the centre of the field to shake hands with Joe Fish and toss for ends.

'Hi,' Joe said. He was chewing gum, and looking very big and tough. I tried to look big and tough too.

'Hi,' I said.

'I want a clean match and no bad language,' said Mr Thompson. Then he grinned. 'When I blow the whistle you can come out fighting.'

It was meant as a joke, but knowing Knocker Lewis I didn't think it was funny!

Joe won the toss, and he decided to play against the wind. We didn't mind that because we thought our smaller players might not last out the second half as well as the Stringy Pants. If we could attack with the wind while we were still fresh we might be able to hold them in the second half. Then, if they had to come forward and put on the pressure, there was always the chance that I would get one in a breakaway, if I could get clear of Joe Fish.

We kicked off.

I played the ball to Joe Small, who slipped it back to John Deacon. As soon as I kicked off I started running down the centre, then veered off to the right, because we knew their left-back was on the slow side. Joe Fish moved across to cover me, and John Deacon slipped a square ball to Harpur Brown who had moved forward into the centre circle. Harpur slipped Gerry Cleland's tackle and hit a long ball behind Joe Fish. I reached the ball first, just on the left-hand side of the penalty box. I could see Hugh Cleland coming slowly out of goal, for a ball which he should have collected anyway. The ball bounced awkwardly in front of me, and I only managed to half hit it. The ball rose lazily in the air and curled over Hugh's head, then bounce, bounce, bounce, it went across the goalmouth and in by the far post.

GOAL! Here is how we scored it:

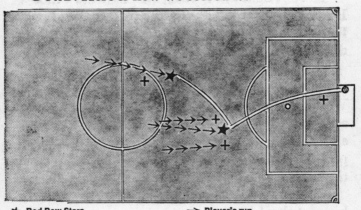

★ Red Row Stars →→ Player's run
✛ Stringy Pants ══ Flight of ball

We had scored straight from the kick-off! Well, almost straight from the kick-off, and exactly as we planned it. One of our basic tactical ideas was to play the ball behind Joe Fish and short of the edge of the area, in the hope that Hugh would be slow coming out. We had done exactly that, and scored.

'Brilliant! Brilliant! 1–0 to us!' John Deacon rushed up and banged me on the back, and the next minute I was knocked over by half our team dashing up to congratulate me.

'Your ball, Joe,' said Hugh Cleland, walking back to pick it out of his net.

Joe Fish pursed his lips, and put his hands on his hips. 'You come out quicker, next time,' he said, and he walked away up the field.

Now they were arguing with each other, and the match had only just begun! Great!

'Keep it tight at the back, Red Row!' I called to Harpur and Cyril, because I knew that the Stringy Pants would come at us like mad, eager to get back the goal they had lost.

That is just what they did!

First it was Neil Collins, waltzing round Scottie Watts on the wing and sending the ball zinging across our goal-mouth. Terence leapt like a tiger and punched the ball out, but he didn't connect properly and Gerry Cleland, following up, blazed the ball high over the open goal. What a let off!

'Come on, Scottie!' I said. 'You've got to keep him out there.'

The next danger came from Knocker Lewis, who brushed Joe Small off the ball and bundled past Dribbler. He booted the ball over Scottie's head and came charging forward on our goal, head down. Terence called out to Harpur to leave the ball, and rushed out to drop on it, just as Knocker was rushing in to score. Thump! They both met the ball together, and Terence somehow held on.

'Watch it, Knocker!' Harpur said.

'Fifty-fifty ball,' said Knocker, but I was pleased to see that he was already looking puffed, after just the one long run.

Terence cleared the ball hard and high, and of course Knocker hadn't run back. It left me with a half-chance, and I was on to it at the speed of light, but Joe Fish came across and slide tackled me, putting the ball away into touch for a throw-in.

'Come on, Knocker!' Joe shouted, in annoyance.

Scuddy Rodgers took the throw-in, and Dribbler took the ball and carried it inside, before slipping a pass to John Deacon, just before Knocker caught up with him. John controlled the ball neatly and slipped it to Scuddy Rodgers, who had moved in behind the back. Scuddy has no ball control, and he was still trying to bring the ball under control when Joe Fish put in a hard tackle, and played the ball out for another throw-in.

Our plans were working. Knocker and the other full-back, Pete Cross, were being exposed by our through passes, and Joe Fish was being overworked at the back covering for them and his stay-on-the-line goalie. The trouble with the St Gabriel's team was that they had piled most of their best players, Gerry Cleland and Neil Collins and Bob Bridges, into the forward line, and left their big slow ones at the back. It meant that as long as they were going forward they looked very strong, but they weren't so good against a quick counter-attack, when the slowness of the two backs put them in all sorts of trouble.

But if I could see that, so could Joe Fish. I heard him shouting orders, and the next thing I knew they had pulled back Bob Bridges. Bob came trotting over to mark me, and Joe himself moved back, as a sweeper behind the two slow backs.

Then Neil Collins got the ball again. He showed it to Dribbler on the left side, switched to his right, and pulled left again. Dribbler ran after him. Neil ran straight on at Scottie, and turned outside him. Out went Scottie's foot, and Neil went down. Dribbler got the ball and was moving clear, when the whistle went.

'Free kick!' Mr Thompson came over and talked to Scottie, then he placed the ball just on the edge of our area where Neil had been fouled.

'Five in the wall!' Terence shouted from the back, and we all took up our positions.

I picked up Joe Fish, moving up-field to the far side of our box, and Harpur Brown took command of the middle, where Gerry Cleland was poised to strike.

Neil Collins took the free kick.

He curled the ball high in the air towards the far post. I saw Joe go past me, and knew that I had lost him.

He rose and headed the ball down and back, into the path of Gerry Cleland, who flicked it towards the corner of the goal.

I don't know how Terence got it! It was a split-second reaction save. He took the ball low down to his left and held it.

Here is what happened:

'Terence!' It was Dribbler Wilson calling. He had moved free of his marker, out on the wing. Terence saw the opportunity, and booted the ball accurately into Dribbler's path. Dribbler took it, controlled it, and squirmed past Knocker Lewis's late lunge. That left him with only Bob Bridges to beat, and meanwhile I was heading up the centre as fast as I could go, knowing that Joe Fish was hopelessly caught up-field.

Dribbler ran on, moving towards the wing, and drawing Bob with him. Then, just when it seemed that he had left it too late, he played a beautiful cross ball straight to my feet. I met it as I ran into the area, and let fly.

WHAM!

It was a super shot, and a goal all the way, but dozy Hugh Cleland chose that moment to show that he is a good goalie, if only he would learn about coming out. Hugh threw himself sideways and punched the ball high in the air. It dropped safely behind the goal for a corner.

I could hardly believe it.

It was a certain score! Little Dribbler had put me clean through, with only the keeper to beat, and I had managed to miss it!

We would have been 2–0 up, with a good chance of holding out when we had to play against the wind in the second half!

'OK, Napper,' Harpur said, as he moved up for the corner. 'Good shot. Hard luck. Keep it up.'

Over came the corner. I went in for it, but Joe Fish beat me in the air again, and headed clear to the mid-field man, who picked out Gerry Cleland with a good through ball. Gerry broke past Cyril and booted the ball ahead, and out came Terence

Prince like an express train to make another of his great smothering saves. You should have seen Cleland's face when he got up! The Stringy Pants had been robbed of another certain goal!

'Look at Dribbler!' I said to Joe Small, as the little kid got the ball again from John Deacon's through pass. Dribbler had just drifted past Knocker Lewis, leaving Knocker panting behind him, before he squared the ball across, high for the near post. Joe Fish came in and beat me to the header.

'Come on, Napper!' Cyril called. 'What's your head for!'

'Cracking nuts!' sneered Knocker Lewis, puffing past me.

'Crack nuts yourself,' I said. 'You just don't like being beaten.'

'You wait till we have the wind, you kids!' said Knocker.

But even without the wind, the Stringy Pants began to take charge. It was then that I realized how important a good goalie is. Terence was having one of his days. Everything that came at him he held, and he even managed to get down to a desperate deflection by Cyril which looked like a goal all the way.

'You're born lucky, you lot,' Joe Fish said, as he moved up for yet another corner.

Over came the ball, and Joe moved past me again, and cracked in another header, which just skimmed the bar. Still, it wasn't a goal, and that was all that mattered.

'Next corner, I'm taking Joe,' Harpur said, and I didn't argue. I was mad about it just the same, because I am good in the air which is how I got my name, Napper. Everybody calls me Napper instead of Bernard, which is my real name. I don't like Bernard and when I'm an international I am going to be called Napper and not Bernard. I can't imagine Bernard McCann playing for Liverpool.

1–0, and time was running out in the first half. The Stringy Pants were on top, despite the score, but Harpur and Cyril were tackling all over the place and Joe Small was using the ball well. Little Dribbler was running rings around Knocker Lewis when he came forward, and really opening up that side of the park. I was pleased, although I would have been happier if we had had more than a one goal lead.

Then the Stringy Pants scored.

It was a simple, silly goal. Knocker Lewis had the ball, out on the wing. He had bundled Dribbler off it, but he was too puffed to run forward. He hit a long hopeful punt into our goal-mouth, where Terence came running out to collect it. Gerry Cleland was rushing in, but Terence seemed to have all the time in the world.

Then things went wrong!

The ball bobbled awkwardly as it hit the turf, just in front of Terence. He was bending to collect it, and instead of coming into his hands, it moved off, struck his elbow, and bobbed forward towards Gerry Cleland, who made a wild lunge at it. Terence dived despairingly, and somehow got one hand to the ball, which ran free, straight into the path of Neil Collins who controlled it, avoided Terence's second attempt, and carefully side-footed the ball into our net!

'Goal!' Knocker yelled, and all the Stringy Pants supporters on the line started jumping about and shouting and singing 'Easy, Easy, make it threesy' which was a bit stupid because they had only equalized, they weren't winning, and they had to get two before they could make it three. Still, it was a goal at the wrong time, just before half time, and worse was to come.

Straight from the kick-off Dribbler made a mistake and lost the ball to a tackle from Gerry Cleland. Gerry found his winger who slipped the ball neatly inside to Joe Fish, who had made a run from the back. Joe took the ball under control, looked round, sized up the position, and unleashed a tremendous shot which crashed into the top corner of our net without Terence being able to do a thing about it.

2–1 to the Stringy Pants.

We kicked off again, and I went on a long run towards the corner flag, with Joe Fish letting me go, because he knew I had no one to come into the centre except Joe Small and Dribbler, neither of whom were likely to be much danger. Joe let me go so far and no farther, then he slide-tackled me, and came away with the ball, which he hit up-field to Neil Collins. Neil took the ball, swung round Scottie Watts for what must have been the tenth time in the game, and sent a high curling ball across the goal which beat Terence all ends up, and landed in the back of our net.

3–1!

The Stringy Pants were still celebrating when the half-time whistle went. We went over to Miss Fellows and sat on the ground, eating our oranges.

'You should have picked Joe up on the second goal, Napper,' Harpur said. 'Don't you think we have enough to do at the back, without their sweeper having a free run?'

'That's quite enough of that, Harpur,' said Miss Fellows. 'You haven't lost the game yet, but you will if you start arguing about it.'

'They're all over us, Miss,' Cyril said glumly.

'Don't be silly,' I said. 'If I hadn't missed one and Terence hadn't dropped the ball it would be two each. Dribbler is going round Knocker every time he gets the ball, and we had them worried for the first twenty minutes. They had to pull Bob Bridges back, remember?'

'Yes,' Cyril said, doubtfully.

'Bet you Bob moves up in the second half,' I said. 'With the wind behind them, and 3–1 up, they'll think it is all over. If I can get one to one with Joe Fish I can beat him. I beat him for the first goal, didn't I?'

'Play the ball on the ground, if you're playing it to Napper!' Harpur advised everyone. I knew what he meant. I hadn't won a single ball in the air against Joe Fish all the first half.

'If I might make a suggestion,' said Miss Fellows, 'I think you would do better if you played the ball to the space in front of Napper, instead of to his feet. When Napper has had to move on to the defence, the centre-half . . . I think you called him Joe, that big one . . . the centre-half has been able to cut him out.'

'And Napper's very quick on the through ball, and Joe is slow to turn . . .' said Terence.

'And Hugh Cleland never leaves his line!' I said. 'That is how we got the first goal. That was our plan, but we haven't been sticking to it.'

'Go for goal in the second half, Napper,' said Terence, grimly. 'Forget about defence. That's up to Cyril, and Harpur, and me.'

Then we went back on to the field to re-start the match, 3–1 down, and facing the wind!

8. Second Half

The Stringy Pants looked very confident as they lined up for the second half, but I had been right about one thing, anyway. Now that they were three goals up, and playing with the wind, Bob Bridges had moved forward, and that meant it was up to me to exploit the slowness of the two backs and the goalie.

The Stringy Pants went straight into the attack. I suppose they thought that if they could get another goal quickly it would put us out for the count. With Bob coming forward, Harpur and Cyril were kept busy in the middle, and that meant that Scottie Watts had to take on Neil Collins on his own. Twice Neil got the ball, and twice he went clear, the first time cutting down to the goal-line and squaring the ball back, only for Cyril to get in a firm clearance, and the second time going inside Scottie and forcing Terence to another good save at the foot of the post.

'Reckon we'll get six,' Knocker Lewis boasted, trotting past me on his way into the attack. I started after him, and then I remembered that that wasn't what I was supposed to do. My job was to stay up-field, keeping Joe Fish occupied, and wait for a break.

Next Harpur burst clear on a long run from defence. He switched the ball out to Joe Small, and kept on running. Joe turned the ball neatly inside with a quick flick and Harpur took it in his stride, brushing past Knocker Lewis and steaming into the penalty area. He was just about to shoot when he lost control of the ball, and Hugh Cleland came rushing out to cover it. Hugh made a quick clearance, and Bob Bridges got the ball and started for our goal, with Harpur hopelessly out of position. I saw what had gone wrong and started off after him. Bob cut inside, checked, and turned the ball across the face of the goal to Gerry Cleland who met it with a hard right-foot drive. Terence parried the ball, which ran loose just as I arrived in the area. I got in a desperate slide tackle and just managed to turn the ball for a goal kick off Neil Collins.

'Come on, St Gabriel's,' Knocker shouted. 'Time we got another one!'

I was puffed out.

'Up you go, Napper,' Cyril said. 'No point in you hanging about in our penalty area, is there? We've got to have somebody to play too, if we do get the ball.'

Terence took the kick and the wind carried the ball high in the air. It bounced awkwardly over Joe Fish's head, straight into my path. It was the first time in ages that I had had the goal in front of me, and I hared after the ball. A quick turn and I was inside Joe Fish, who had come racing back. For once Hugh Cleland came out, and I went to chip him, then changed my mind and slid the ball round him. Hugh dived desperately, but I evaded him, and ran on across the front of the goal, before side-footing the ball into the net!

GOAL!

And the next minute . . . CRUNCH!

I felt something hurtle against my legs, and I went down in the middle of the penalty area. It was Knocker Lewis, lunging in with one of his late tackles.

'That'll teach you, Napper,' he said, getting up.

The referee had turned back to the centre of the field when the ball went into the net, and he had missed Knocker's late tackle. I limped back to the middle, for the centre. My ankle was very sore where Knocker had scraped his boot against it as we went down. Still, I had scored!

3–2 to the Stringy Pants.

'Come on, St Gabriel's!' Joe Fish was urging them on to the attack, but then little Dribbler began to take a hand. He turned Knocker inside out twice, making the big fellow look a fool, and each time he laid off a good ball. The first one went to John Deacon, who fluffed it and played the ball into touch. The second came waist-high to me. I controlled it, and tapped it inside to John Deacon, who played a swift one-two with me, slipping the ball behind Joe Fish. I reached it on the edge of the area, and slammed in a shot which Hugh Cleland got down to save at the foot of the post. This was the way we did it:

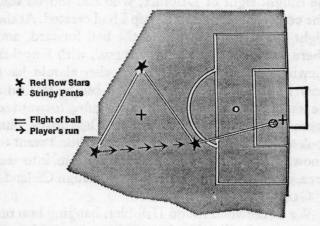

Red Row Stars
Stringy Pants

Flight of ball
Player's run

After that, the Stringy Pants went back on to the attack. Gradually they were getting on top of us, as our smaller players began to tire, but still they couldn't beat Terence. He tipped over a header from Bob Bridges, and cut out two of Neil Collins's crosses, the second one right off the top of Gerry Cleland's head.

After the second of Terence's saves, he played the ball out to Cyril Small on the right. Cyril had been staying back right through the game, but this time he put his head down and tried a run, because he could see that the Stringy Pants were all backing off him, expecting him to make a big clearance. He started forward, and I moved out to the wing, taking Joe Fish with me, hoping he could play a long ball for me to chase on to. But Cyril saw something better than that. Out of the corner of his eye he caught sight of Dribbler, who had moved into the centre, heading for the gap I had created. At the right moment Cyril slipped the ball forward, and there was Dribbler heading for goal, with Knocker Lewis nowhere to be seen. Knocker should have been marking Dribbler, of course, but by this time he was much more concerned with going forward to score goals, and anyway Dribbler had made him look a fool several times, so Knocker didn't want to know. Dribbler took the ball coolly, ran into the area, and slotted the ball neatly past Hugh Cleland!

GOAL!

We all crowded round Dribbler, banging him on the back and telling him it was the greatest goal ever.

3–3, and we were back in the game, when it had looked almost impossible.

'Dribbler's in the team for good!' Harpur said to me, as we ran back to the centre. 'Did you see how cleverly he moved into the space after you drew Joe Fish out to the wing?'

'Look at Knocker's face,' I said. 'He's gone pale again.'

Harpur frowned. When Knocker goes pale it means he has lost his temper, and when Knocker loses his temper, it means trouble.

It was Dribbler who ran into it.

Terence had cleared a long ball from his goal-mouth and, for the first time in the game, I beat Joe Fish to it in the air, and glanced a header sideways to Dribbler. Dribbler took the ball in his stride, checked, and went to move outside Knocker, who had come panting across to him.

WHAM!

Knocker swung into the tackle, catching Dribbler just below the knee. Dribbler went down like a ninepin, and the referee's whistle blew furiously.

Knocker got a lecture from Mr Thompson, but he didn't get sent off. I don't think he minded, for I saw him grinning as he ran back to take up his position for the free kick. Dribbler wasn't grinning. He limped out to the wing, and stood testing his leg.

'Should we substitute him?' Harpur asked. 'It's up to you, Napper. It looks as if Knocker is out to get him, doesn't it? He's been making Knocker look foolish, and Knocker doesn't like that.'

I thought about it. Dribbler was so small that he hadn't been considered for the team when we first started, but now that he had managed to get into the team, he had been absolutely brilliant, running rings round the defence and scoring a great goal. I was pretty certain that Knocker wouldn't go for him again and risk being sent off, and I knew that little Dribbler standing on one leg was a better player than Mark Bellow, wandering around the pitch on two. The player we wanted was Harry

Haxwell, but he was under suspension, though by this time he had arrived behind Hugh Cleland's goal, and was cheering like mad every time we went on the attack. I could see he wanted to be on the team now, and we were certainly missing him. But Harry's problems would have to wait. My problem was whether to keep Dribbler on and risk Knocker having another go at him, or take him off and put on big Mark. Nobody would trip Mark, but then nobody would need to, for Mark was expert at falling over himself, without assistance.

'I'm keeping Dribbler on, Harpur,' I said.

Harpur shrugged, and went to take the free kick. He placed the ball and then he tweaked his left ear. Secret Sign Number Eight!

I made my way across the goal to the near post, drawing Joe Fish near me.

Cyril had seen the ear-tweak Secret Sign, and he started to trot up-field, drawing Bob Bridges across towards the far post. The two smaller Stringy Pants' defenders in the centre lay in close to the goalkeeper, knowing how slow Hugh was to come out. The goal-mouth was packed, but there was about to be a great big gap at the edge of the area, created by our Secret Plan.

Harpur ran up to take the kick. As he started running, so did I. I ran straight at him, and I could feel Joe Fish pounding behind me, as I came out of the penalty area. At the same moment Cyril moved towards the far post, and Bob went after him. The other Stringy Pants who had been expecting a long ball for me to try a header, didn't know what to do. They stood stock still.

Harpur played the ball straight at me, and kept on running.

He went past me in a blur of speed, just as I flicked the ball and Joe Fish crashed into me. I got no more than a touch to it, and there it was, on the edge of the area, right in Harpur's path, with Hugh Cleland caught amongst the players who had been covering him.

Harpur didn't hesitate.

He drilled the ball into the top corner of the net.

Here is how Secret Plan Number Eight worked:

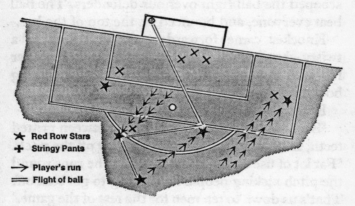

Red Row Stars

Stringy Pants

Player's run

Flight of ball

4–3 to Red Row Stars!

Back surged the Stringy Pants into attack, but

now they weren't so confident. Gerry Cleland blazed the ball wide from a good position. Neil Collins got himself caught off-side. Bob Bridges crashed one into the side netting. Terence saved from the left-winger, and then smothered a close-in drive from Knocker Lewis.

Time was ticking away.

'How long, Sir?' I asked Mr Thompson.

'Time enough,' he said.

Joe Fish moved up into the attack, and had a header saved by Terence. Then Terence dropped a shot from Willy Savidge, and Cyril somehow got back to scoop the ball off the line. John Deacon gave away a free kick on the edge of the area, and we all went back to make a line. Joe Fish took the kick and scooped the ball right over our defenders. The ball beat everyone, and bounced on the top of the bar.

Knocker came forward again, and sent in a twisty shot, which Terence smothered. Knocker followed up, and caught Terence with his trailing boot, and the whistle went!

Knocker was sent off!

'Serve him right,' said Joe Fish, between gritted teeth, as we watched Knocker walking off the pitch. 'Fat lot of use crying about it now. If he runs round the pitch kicking people he is going to get sent off. That's us down to ten men for the rest of the game.'

'We've been the same, since he kicked Dribbler,' I pointed out, and it was true. Dribbler was almost useless on the wing.

'Bring on your sub,' said Joe.

'Have you seen my sub?' I said, and Joe grinned.

The Stringy Pants weren't finished. They launched a series of desperate attacks, with Joe moving further and further up field, in the search for a last-minute equalizer.

That gave me my chance.

Terence had the ball, and I was all alone on the half-way line!

'Terence!'

He saw me, and kicked.

I collected the ball in the centre circle and set off for goal. I knew another goal now, with only seconds to go, would seal the match.

I was clear of the defenders.

Hugh dashed out of his area, and seeing I was going to beat him to it, dived at me, smothering the ball in his arms!

The whistle went for the free kick.

Hugh started back for his goal.

He should have got the red card but Mr Thompson didn't send him off, probably because Mr Cleland had turned up to watch.

He had cheated me by handling the ball outside his area ... but I had a trick worth two of that. Hugh shouldn't have turned his back!

I grabbed the ball, placed it, and glanced at Mr Thompson. He saw what I was going to do, and nodded.

'Hugh!' Joe Fish yelled, suddenly waking up.

Hugh had been ambling back to goal, congratulating himself on giving away a free kick for handling the ball outside his area, and thereby saving a certain goal. He turned round when he heard Joe Fish's yell, just in time to see the ball streaking past him on its way to the back of the Stringy Pants' net.

GOAL!

5–3 TO RED ROW STARS!

I had scored a hat-trick!

'You are a fool, Cleland,' Mr Thompson said, picking the ball out of the back of the net.

'Sir! Sir! Napper cheated! That's no goal. He didn't give me time to get back to my net. I wasn't ready!'

'*You* cheated, Cleland. You deprived McCann of a perfectly good goal by handling the ball outside your area. Then you stood around congratulating yourself. He took the free kick quickly, which he is quite entitled to do. If you didn't cover your goal, that is your fault. McCann got the goal he deserved, and a very well-taken one too.'

Hugh went back to his goal, crimson in the face.

'Great goal, Napper!' said Terence. 'That was real quick-thinking!'

Joe Fish took the kick-off himself, in a last attempt to get the Stringy Pants back into the game. He and Neil Collins launched an attack down the wing, but the ball ended up in touch, and then the final whistle went.

5–3 to Red Row Stars!

We had WON!

Everybody shouted and cheered and danced about, even Harry Haxwell, who was running around banging us all on the back as though he'd never been happier in his life. Miss Fellows had a big grin on her face.

'Three cheers for the Stringy ... I mean St Gabriel's,' I called out, catching sight of Miss Fellows' face as I was about to say 'Stringy Pants'.

We gave three cheers.

'Three cheers for Red Row Stars!' said Joe Fish.

All the Stringy Pants cheered, and some of us were almost cheering as well.

Our team had turned out to be better than we had ever thought it could be. We had beaten the Stringy Pants. We weren't the Red Row kids any more. We were Red Row Stars, the Champions of Barnleck.

Miss Fellows had orange juice and sandwiches and cream buns waiting for us in the hall, to celebrate our first big match, although it wouldn't have been much of a celebration if we had lost. When we had eaten everything up she said: 'Next term, we'll have to see about entering a team in the Junior League.'

'Bet we win it!' said Terence at once.

'Course we will,' said Cyril.

'Why "of course", Cyril?' asked Miss Fellows.

And we all answered her, in chorus:

'Because ... WE ARE THE CHAMPIONS! WE
ARE THE CHAMPIONS!'
And it was true!

FOOTBALL NOTES

By E. Fellows (Ms)

This term has seen the formation of a football team at Red Row School, for the first time. The boys responsible for this innovation were Prince, McCann, Brown and Small. The following players took part:

Prince, Terence is a brave and agile goalkeeper, and has played a leading part in organizing the team.

Small, Cyril A great enthusiast, Cyril is a mainstay of our defence.

Small, Joseph Ball control is poor, but Joseph has the ability to do simple things well.

Watts, Andrew 'Scottie' tends to be slow and ponderous on occasions, but has stuck manfully to his task.

Forbes, Duncan Tenacious, but small. Duncan will improve with time.

Brown, Harpur A thoughtful player. His 'Secret Plans' are our secret weapon. Could perhaps introduce a little more aggression into his play.

Scott, Peter There is room for improvement in Peter's game. He does not use his height and weight.

McCann, Bernard 'Napper' is our leading goalscorer. Captain of the team, is at times a little hot-headed.

Rodgers, Scudamore 'Scuddy' is rather small, and tends to fade out of the game.

Bellow, Mark Shows little appetite for the game.

Wilson, Donald 'Dribbler' has proved a great success. He is a 'Star' for the future.

Haxwell, Harold A strong player, who must learn to control his temper. Harold has, as yet, no sense of obligation to his team mates.

Our thanks are due to Mr Hogan who opened the hall for us and to the Mums (and Dads?) who helped sew our famous Red Row Shirts.

E. Fellows (Ms)

Napper Strikes Again

by Martin Waddell

After an eventful first season, Napper McCann and the Red Row Stars are back again and determined to win the local Youth League Cup. Now in their second season, Napper and his team are convinced they can win the Cup, but they meet so many problems that they begin to wonder if they'll ever get through in one piece.

Napper's Golden Goals

by Martin Waddell

Napper McCann, Captain and demon goal-scorer of the Red Row Stars, is trying to hold his team together in very difficult circumstances. Can Napper cope with muddles caused by new 'star' player Boomer? Can Red Row win the Cup?

Napper's Big Match

by Martin Waddell

Will Napper McCann's promising football career come to an end after the collapse of the Red Row Stars, or can he become Demon Goalscorer for another team? Napper's determined efforts to carry on playing end in near disaster, but an unexpected chance to try out for a new team gives him hope. Competition to join the side is fierce, and Napper faces one of his toughest challenges yet.

Napper Super-Sub

by Martin Waddell

Napper McCann and his team-mates have a tough challenge if the Warne County Colts are to make it into the Premier Division of the newly formed Brontely League. But how is Napper going to become a star when he spends so much time on the subs' bench? Is Napper's football career about to end just as he makes it into real competition?

The Wacky World of Wesely Baker

by Gene Kemp

Wesley's life is hard enough as it is. All his family are fitness freaks, while he would prefer to write stories in peace. And Agnes Potter Higgins, the maddest girl in the school, is in love with him and follows him EVERYWHERE! But when Dad decides that Wesley will be the sports day champion and Mrs Warble casts him as St George in the school play (with Agnes as the princess), his world really begins to turn upside down.

'No one writes with more insight into the primary school classroom, its pupils or its teachers than this author' – *The Irish Times*

READ MORE IN PUFFIN

For children of all ages, Puffin represents quality and variety – the very best in publishing today around the world.

For complete information about books available from Puffin – and Penguin – and how to order them, contact us at the appropriate address below. Please note that for copyright reasons the selection of books varies from country to country.

On the worldwide web: www.puffin.co.uk

In the United Kingdom: Please write to *Dept. EP, Penguin Books Ltd, Bath Road, Harmondsworth, West Drayton, Middlesex UB7 ODA*

In the United States: Please write to *Consumer Sales, Penguin USA, P.O. Box 999, Dept. 17109, Bergenfield, New Jersey 07621-0120*. VISA and MasterCard holders call 1-800-253-6476 to order Penguin titles

In Canada: Please write to *Penguin Books Canada Ltd, 10 Alcorn Avenue, Suite 300, Toronto, Ontario M4V 3B2*

In Australia: Please write to *Penguin Books Australia Ltd, P.O. Box 257, Ringwood, Victoria 3134*

In New Zealand: Please write to *Penguin Books (NZ) Ltd, Private Bag 102902, North Shore Mail Centre, Auckland 10*

In India: Please write to *Penguin Books India Pvt Ltd, 706 Eros Apartments, 56 Nehru Place, New Delhi 110 019*

In the Netherlands: Please write to *Penguin Books Netherlands bv, Postbus 3507, NL-1001 AH Amsterdam*

In Germany: Please write to *Penguin Books Deutschland GmbH, Metzlerstrasse 26, 60594 Frankfurt am Main*

In Spain: Please write to *Penguin Books S. A., Bravo Murillo 19, 1° B, 28015 Madrid*

In Italy: Please write to *Penguin Italia s.r.l., Via Felice Casati 20, I–20124 Milano*

In France: Please write to *Penguin France S. A., 17 rue Lejeune, F–31000 Toulouse*

In Japan: Please write to *Penguin Books Japan, Ishikiribashi Building, 2–5–4, Suido, Bunkyo-ku, Tokyo 112*

In South Africa: Please write to *Longman Penguin Southern Africa (Pty) Ltd, Private Bag X08, Bertsham 2013*